MW00949559

For Malcolm — M.F.

For Peter and Jeremy — J.H.

Ducks Away! was originally published in Australia by Scholastic Australia Pty Limited in 2016.
This US edition was published under license from Scholastic Australia Pty Limited.

Library of Congress Cataloging-in-Publication Data
Names: Fox, Mem, author. | Horacek, Judy, illustrator. | Title: Ducks away! / by Mem Fox ; illustrated by Judy Horacek.
Description: First American edition. | New York : Scholastic Press, an imprint of Scholastic Inc., 2018. | "Ducks Away! was originally published in Australia by Scholastic Australia Pty Limited in 2016" — Copyright page. Summary: One by one five little ducklings tumble off the bridge into the river below — and mother duck follows them. Identifiers: LCCN 2016059276
ISBN 9781338185669 (jacketed hardcover) | Subjects: LCSH: Ducks — Juvenile fiction. CYAC: Ducks — Fiction. | Counting. | Classification: LCC PZ7.F8373 Du 2018 | DDC [E] — dc23 LC record available at https://lccn.loc.gov/2016059276

10 9 8 7 6 5 4 3 2 1 18 19 20 21 22

Printed in China 137
This edition first printing, February 2018

One fine day, a mother duck
waddled onto a bridge.

A fluffy yellow duckling
followed right behind her.

Actually, it was two little ducks.

No, it was three little ducks.

Wait! It was four little ducks.

What? It was five little ducks,

except just then . . .

a sudden gust of wind swept the last little

duck right into the river below!

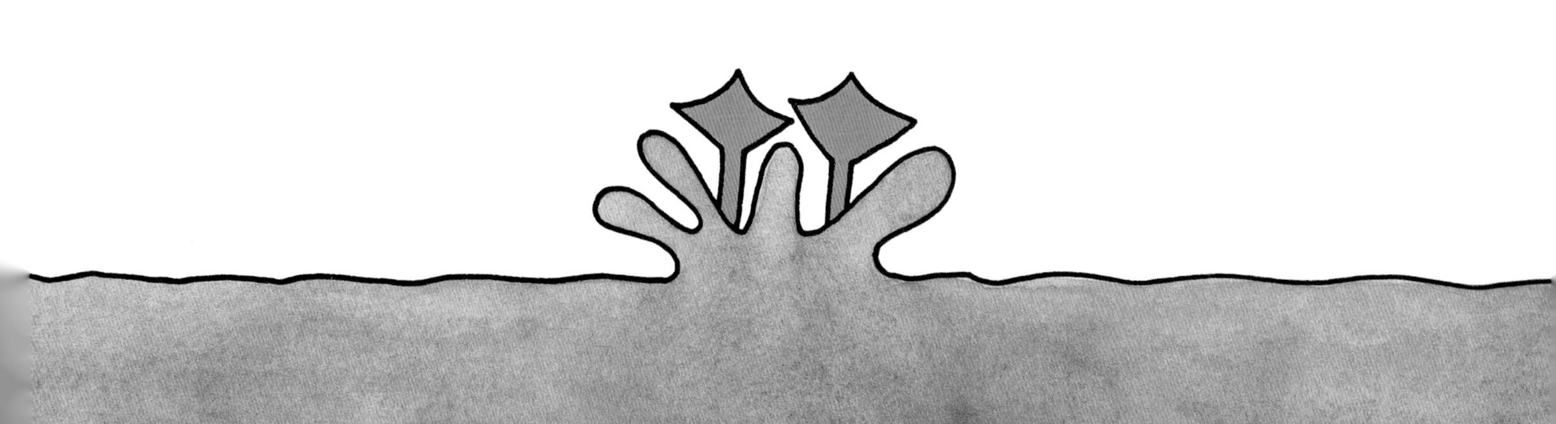

"Oh no!" quacked Mother Duck.

"What should I do?

Where should I go,

with four on the bridge

and one below?"

One of the other little ducks
decided to take a look,
and *he* toppled into the river below!

"Oh no!" quacked Mother Duck.

"What should I do?

Where should I go,

with three on the bridge

and two below?"

Then another little duck peered over the edge,

and *she* toppled into the river below!

"Oh no!" quacked Mother Duck.
"What should I do?
Where should I go,
with two on the bridge
and three below?"

Then another little duck peeked over the edge,

and *she* toppled into the river below!

"Oh no!" quacked Mother Duck.

"What should I do?

Where should I go,

with one on the bridge

and four below?"

Then the last little duck foolishly lost his footing . . .

and *he* tumbled into the river as well!

Mother Duck looked down.

The five little ducks looked up.

And Mother Duck
flew to the river below!

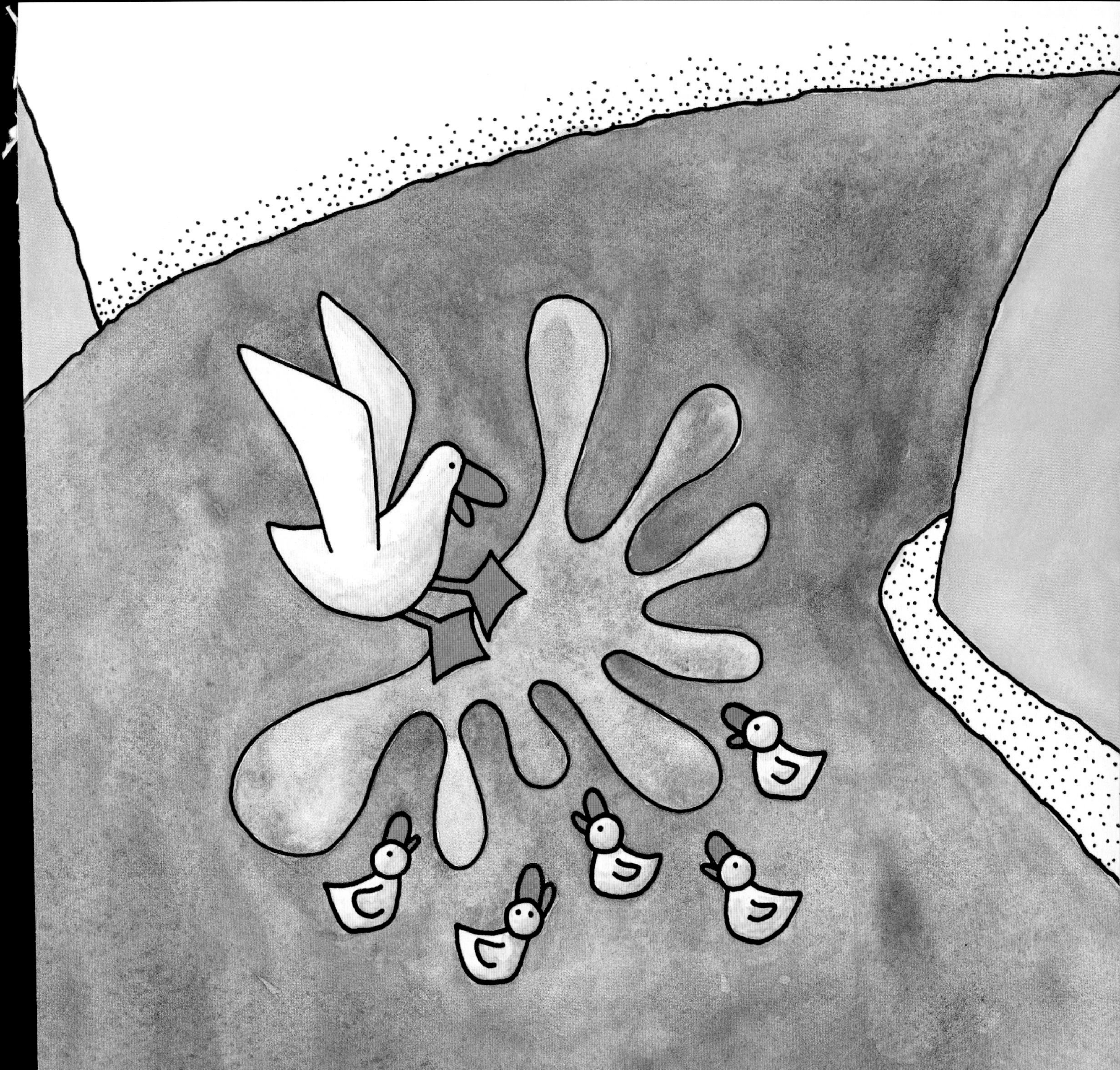

“Quack,” said the five little ducks.

"You're BACK!"